Is Grandpa Wearing a Suit?

Is Grandpa Wearing a Suit?

Amelie Fried / Illustrated by Jacky Gleich

 Books

Alhambra, California

"*I*s Grandpa wearing a suit?" Bruno wonders, as he stands on his tiptoes, trying to peek inside the casket.

"Grandpa has left us," says Sammie.

"That can't be right," Bruno thinks. "Grandpa hasn't gone anywhere... he's lying right here!"

Bruno isn't tall enough to see inside. All he can see are the soles of a pair of black leather dress shoes sticking up over the casket's edge. Grandpa used to wear only boots.

"If Grandpa's wearing dress shoes," he thinks, "he must be wearing a suit!"

*A*ll at once, someone lifts Bruno up high so he can get a closer look at his grandfather. He *is* wearing a suit! Grandpa's hands are folded over his chest. His eyes are closed.

"Grandpa's still alive," Bruno exclaims. "He's only sleeping!"

After a while, Bruno is set back down on the floor. Someone strokes his head, murmuring, "Poor boy."

Bruno's parents discuss whether he should be allowed to attend the burial. For Bruno, the word "burial" means something like "digging a hole." When Bruno plays in the sand, he likes to dig a large hole, put some things in it, then cover it up to hide the things. But if "burial" really means "digging a hole," Bruno wonders, "Will someone have to dig a hole to hide Grandpa?"

"I am going to the burial!" Bruno cries out.

A crowd of people are walking toward the cemetery alongside the casket. Bruno's four uncles are serving as pallbearers. Behind follow Bruno's father and mother, Sammie, Auntie Mickey, and lots of other aunts and uncles who Bruno doesn't even know. It's pouring out, and Bruno is wearing a raincoat. This makes him feel good.

The uncles who are carrying the casket walk very slowly. The band is playing mournful music. Bruno feels he is about to cry. Suddenly, an uncle trips on a stone, steps in a puddle, and splashes water on everyone around him. Bruno can't help but laugh, but he is shushed quiet by the adults, who glare at him disapprovingly. Finally, the procession stops. A priest starts reading a long, dull eulogy for Bruno's grandfather. Bruno sees his dad sobbing. When Bruno cries, the adults will comfort him. "But who will comfort the adults when *they* cry?" wonders Bruno.

*T*he priest finishes the eulogy. Some strong-looking men use a strap to lower the casket into a large hole in the ground. "What is Grandpa doing in there? Does he hear the priest's prayers and Auntie Mickey's crying?" Bruno asks himself. Auntie Mickey loves to have a good cry. She can easily cry her eyes out over the smallest thing. Grandpa used to laugh at her.

Bruno doesn't understand what it means to "die". "It's like sleeping," Sammie once told him, "but you never wake up." Is that true? Sammie liked to kid Bruno, so Bruno doesn't know whether to believe him or not. Not long ago, Sammie said, "Look at that flying cow!" When Bruno looked up to see the flying cow, Sammie took a huge bite out of Bruno's ice cream cone.

*A*fter the funeral, everyone walks to a restaurant. Crying must make people hungry, because today they eat a lot of meat and potatoes. Crying must also make people thirsty, because they drink a lot of beer, too. After eating and drinking, some people tell funny stories about Grandpa. Bruno concludes that lots of eating and drinking can help you put sad things out of your mind.

"Grandpa must be very happy now," Bruno's dad says, drying his tears.

The others ate meat and potatoes, but Bruno had only a little bread with mustard on it. He likes bread with mustard. "The more mustard you eat, the more foolish you'll be," Grandpa always said. Grandpa is no longer here, and the other adults don't have time to scold Bruno.

Bruno's father and mother are still very happy on the way home at night. Bruno can't understand why there was never a celebration like this while Grandpa was alive.

"*W*here is Grandpa now?" asks Bruno several days later.

"In the ground," says Sammie.

"In heaven," says Dad.

"So which place is it?" asks Bruno, looking at them.

"Both," his mother says.

After hearing these answers, Bruno is upset. He runs to the barn to hide. He knows perfectly well that it's impossible for a person to be in two places at once. It would, for example, be impossible for him to be in both the kitchen and the barn at the same time! Before, whenever there was something he couldn't understand, he always ran to Grandpa for an answer. Now Grandpa was gone, and nobody could say exactly where he had gone. Bruno runs up to his grandfather's room. He thinks: "Maybe Grandpa has come back... maybe the adults were wrong and he's not dead at all!" Bruno finds everything in Grandpa's room just as he left it. Something *is* different, however: it's tidier. Grandpa must have come back to clean his room. "But where has he gone?" Bruno wonders.

*B*runo sits on the big old armchair by the window. Grandpa often sat here reading books about boats. He once dreamed of becoming a sailor. In the end however he, like his father before him, became a farmer. Bruno's dad is also a farmer. Sometimes Bruno wonders whether he would like to be a farmer when he grows up.

Bruno is holding a wooden boat that Grandpa brought back from a journey, the only trip he ever took. He traveled to Genoa. Bruno doesn't know where Genoa is. What he does know is that there is a port there and many boats. Every time Bruno asked for the small wooden boat, Grandpa would say, "One day you'll inherit it." "Inherit" means that a person can get another person's things when he or she dies. Now that Grandpa has died, the boat belongs to Bruno. He holds it carefully in his hands and examines it, touching it gently. Then he puts it under his sweater. He stares out the window for a long time.

"*H*ow can Grandpa be both in the ground and in heaven at the same time?" Bruno asks his mother.

Bruno's mother sighs, clasps her hands, and says, "I don't think you'd understand."

"I'll understand it if you explain it to me!" protests Bruno.

"All right," she says. "Grandpa's body is in the grave. But his soul has gone to heaven. He's with God now."

"What's a 'soul' ?" asks Bruno.

"I think you're a bit too young to understand," says his mother, kissing his forehead.

"Is a 'soul' the other Grandpa?"

Mom pauses and says, "You could think of it that way."

One day, Sammie finds Bruno in the kitchen. Bruno quickly hides something behind his back. Sammie grabs Bruno's arm and discovers a slice of bread with mustard in his hand.

"Why is the mustard side facing downwards?" asks Sammie.

"So Grandpa up in heaven can't see it," says Bruno.

"You are really a dum-dum..." says Sammie, as he laughs and runs out of the kitchen.

Bruno takes a bite of his mustard bread and thinks that maybe his grandfather is too far away to see it clearly. Grandpa was very nearsighted.

Bruno can't understand some of the words the adults are using, like "soul" and "God".

"Is the soul alive in heaven?" he asks his dad.

"I think so."

"So Grandpa isn't *really* dead."

"Grandpa *is* dead. But he still lives on in our memories," replies his dad.

Bruno nods his head. He agrees. All he has to do is remember his grandfather, and he will appear.

"But what if I forget what Grandpa looks like?" asks Bruno.

*A*t night, Bruno's dad gives him a small cardboard box. Bruno opens it very carefully. Inside is a photograph of Grandpa waving his tan hat and smiling. Looking at the photo, Bruno suddenly feels sad. He presses the picture to his heart and before long, he falls asleep.

One day, Bruno sits by the roadside looking at the lake. He misses his grandpa again. Grandpa once told Bruno he would teach him how to fish. They decided they would go together when Sunday came. But many a Sunday came and went...

Bruno suddenly feels angry that Grandpa didn't keep his promise before going to heaven. How could he leave without a word, without even a goodbye? How could Grandpa leave him alone like this?

Now Bruno would never learn how to fish because only his grandpa knew how. In fact, there were lots of things that only Grandpa knew how to do, like how to make a whistle from a twig, how to softly approach fawns eating grass, and how to recognize different species of fungi in the forest— these were the kinds of things that Bruno could only learn from his grandpa. "But now Grandpa's dead and he's never coming back..."

Bruno doesn't feel angry anymore, he feels sad. For the first time since Grandpa's death, he cries.

*B*runo's father is in the house, writing. Bruno tugs at his sleeve and asks, "Dad, when will I die?"

Bruno's dad turns to look at his son. "We don't know. Nobody knows when he or she, or other people, will die."

"But I want to know," says Bruno.

"Actually, it's best that we don't know. Do you know the old Native American saying?"

Bruno shakes his head and opens his eyes wide. He wants to know everything about Native Americans.

"Live each day to the fullest, as if it were your last."

Bruno doesn't completely understand, but he likes the way it sounds.

"How many souls are there up in heaven?" he asks.

"Don't worry, there will be room for yours," his dad replies with a smile.

"But what if heaven gets too full?"

Bruno's father thinks for a while and says, "Some people believe in reincarnation. They believe that the soul returns to Earth in another form."

"Do *you* believe that?" asks Bruno.

"I really don't know," says his father, shrugging his shoulders.

*I*mmediately after Grandpa's death, the family stops doing some of the things they usually do. Weeks later, however, everything is back to normal. Bruno's father and mother are back at their farm work. Sammie goes to school every day, and plays soccer every Saturday. Bruno helps his mother at home, the same as before, watering the vegetable garden, washing clothes, and gathering eggs in the henhouse. At first, Bruno feels a pain in his chest. He thinks that maybe there's a hole in his heart. Every night before going to bed, he looks at his grandpa's picture and says, "I'll never forget you."

He makes this promise every day. Sometimes he can feel Grandpa smiling at him from far away.

Bruno feels the hole in his heart slowly closing up.

One day when Bruno has some free time, he goes to visit his grandpa's grave. He carries a small bucket with him, which he uses to water the plants and flowers on the plot. First he clears away all the withered flowers and leaves, and sweeps away some needles from under a pine tree. Then he sits down by the grave, and thinks about the things he used to do with his grandfather. Sometimes, he seems to hear Grandpa's voice, though he knows it's really just the wind blowing through the branches and leaves.

At first Bruno visits Grandpa in the cemetery quite often. Over time, he goes there less and less frequently.

One day, his father says, "It's been a year since Grandpa passed away..."

Bruno realizes that the pain in his heart has been gradually lessening. In Bruno's heart, Grandpa is always smiling — just like in the picture. "If Grandpa is happy now, maybe I should start being happier, too," Bruno thinks.

Auntie Mickey's tummy has been getting bigger and bigger. At first Bruno didn't pay it much mind, but everyone else has been discussing her swelling tummy, sometimes over lunch, sometimes at night as they chat by the fire. One day, Sammie rushes into Bruno's room and says, "Auntie Mickey's had a baby!"

Several days later, Auntie Mickey visits Bruno's family, holding a baby wearing a diaper that's too big for him. All Bruno can see are two little red shoes sticking out of the big diaper. When Bruno stands on his tiptoes to get a better look, someone lifts him up close to the baby. The baby's rosy face is wrinkly. He gets ready to cry, flailing his tiny fists defiantly.

"Maybe Grandpa has come back!" says Bruno's mother, looking at the little baby.

Bruno is surprised to hear this, and has another look at the baby.

"No, this can't be Grandpa," Bruno says. "Grandpa is much bigger. And Grandpa's wearing a suit and black dress shoes."

Heryin Books

1033 E. Main St., #202, Alhambra, CA 91801
editor@heryin.com   www.heryin.com

HAT OPA EINEN ANZUG AN?
Copyright © Carl Hanser Verlag München Wien 1997
Translation copyright © 2007 by Heryin Books

Library of Congress Cataloging-in-Publication Data
Fried, Amelie, 1958-[Hat Opa einen Anzug an? English]
Is Grandpa Wearing a Suit? / written by Amelie Fried;
illustrated by Jacky Gleich. — 1st English ed. p. cm.
Summary: Bruno's grandfather has passed away. Bruno
participates in the funeral with the grown-ups, but doesn't think
his grandfather has died, he's just sleeping!
I. Gleich, Jacky, 1964 - ill. II. Title.   2007007226
ISBN : 978-0-9787-5504-1